MIRA NIKOLOVA

Tigers in Athens
and other stories

MIRA NIKOLOVA
TIGERS IN ATHENS
and other stories

ISBN (UK): 978-1-0369-0038-0

© Copyright MIRA NIKOLOVA

Cover Illustrator: Yana Popova

Creative Assistants: Marina Shileva-Slavchev,
    Pavlina Kostarakou

All rights reserved

No part of this publication may be reproduced, translated, stored in a retrieval system, or transmitted, in any form or by any means, electronic, mechanical, photocopying, microfilming, recording, or otherwise, without the prior permission in writing of the Author.

London, November 2024

Mira Nikolova Publishing
studio@miranikolova.com

With special thanks to:

Ilko Nikolov
Petya Nikolova
Mariya Nikolova
Marina Shileva-Slavchev
Pavlina Kostarakou
Yana Popova

Contents

Snow 9
Perfect Ghost 19
Tigers in Athens 29
The Strange Aquarium 39
Fog 47
The Run 57
Rose Gold 65
Kali Orexi 77
Land of Gods 91

Snow

The snow started falling at exactly 10 am on Sunday morning, just like the weather forecast had predicted. I eagerly peeked through the window with anticipation and was thrilled at the sight. At first, the grey sky sprinkled delicate little snowflakes. Shy and apprehensive, they pirouetted in the air and then landed softly on the ground. Their graceful dance slowly brought the motionless world to life. Stirred by their elegant performance, the empty streets began to awake. People in thick winter coats and warm hats strolled along the white pavements, and an occasional car sluggishly rolled down the snow-covered road.

I was sitting on the sofa by the window sipping a hot coffee and munching on some clementines, my eyes glued to the mesmerising spectacle outside. Gradually, the snowflakes grew bigger —

more confident. They came in swarms and, flying in synchrony, wove ephemeral drawings in the air, then raced each other violently and fearlessly hurled themselves to the ground. This symphony of movement became more elaborate, more passionate, and I felt the urge to get closer to the stage.

I put on a black wool coat and a white fur hat, then headed to the river. I passed the boathouses and watched the long queue by the German bratwurst stand that was now beautifully decorated with fairy lights. People with animated faces and rosy cheeks were sipping hot cocoa and chatting restlessly. The spicy scent of mulled wine mixed with agitated conversations and sincere laughter drifted leisurely in the air among the snowflakes.

Once I moved away from the pier, everything became hushed as if the snow had swallowed all sounds and a white impenetrable silence enveloped the path. The snow fell in chunky flakes that fluttered around me like tiny exotic birds, flapping their wings languidly before nesting in the black wool of my coat. The grey river stretched along the path, emanating an icy silver glow that blended with the skyline in the distance.

I had walked along this route countless times, but now it looked brand new. Dazzling whiteness surrounded me while black tree branches dusted with snow swayed above my head. Blinded by this fairy-tale-like scenery I felt ecstatic. My feet no longer seemed to touch the ground as I floated in a whirlpool of snowflakes. I walked wrapped up in this hazy euphoria for what must have been an hour when I finally realised that my feet were completely soaked, heavy and felt like ice.

When I got home, I took a long hot shower and tried to warm up with a bowl of tomato soup and sourdough toast, but I was still shivering. The cold had quietly seeped into my bones. I suddenly felt sad and drained as if the snow had sucked all the exhilaration and energy out of my body. I tried to retrace my steps mentally to see where along the road I could have lost my earlier excitement but all I could visualise was a fierce avalanche that froze my thoughts. I gave up and sat down by the window with a book and a glass of Monkey Shoulder.

Outside, the snow-covered town glimmered in the blue dusk light. A snowman had appeared in the middle of the playground across the road, standing proudly with his carrot nose and black button eyes and grin. There was something unusual about him but I couldn't quite pinpoint it. His body was formed of three perfectly shaped spheres that were connected so seamlessly that he looked weightless and agile... it was as if he was made of smoke rather than snow. His eyes gleamed under the streetlamp and I had the feeling that he was looking straight at me. Suddenly, he raised his hand and waved at me with his jelly worm fingers. I thought that the whiskey must be getting to my head, but no matter how many times I blinked and opened my eyes, the snowman was still there waving. Overwhelmed with curiosity, I put on a beige oversized scarf and my sheepskin boots and rushed towards the playground.

"Good evening," the snowman said as I approached him. Lost for words, I just stared at him, my mind a cloud of confusion.

"You're probably surprised that I can talk, but the truth is, a lot of snowmen can talk," he continued. "I was getting a bit bored sitting here on my own, so I decided to wave at you."

The evening air was chilly and I regretted not bringing a coat.

"I would love to stay here and talk to you, but I'm so cold," I finally spoke. The snowman's button mouth formed a pleasant smile.

"I don't want to impose, but could we possibly have a drink at your place if it's not too much trouble?" Things were already taking a strange course, so I could only agree.

The snowman followed me into the building. He moved effortlessly like a water snake gliding smoothly along the placid surface of a lake. As we took the lift to the third floor, I was relieved not to run into any neighbours as the sight of the snowman might have stunned them. Once we entered my warm apartment, I feared that the snowman might begin to melt, but somehow, the snow that he was made of stayed intact. We sat by the coffee table, glasses filled with whiskey in hand, while he talked about the children who built him. He noticed the piano in the corner of the living room and asked me if he could play something. I had no reason to object, so he settled in front of the instrument.

What followed was music so exquisite and pure that it couldn't have belonged to this world. His jelly worm fingers touched the keys with such grace and affection that the alien sounds they produced seemed to materialize into tangible waves of emotion that flowed through me and I no longer felt cold. The melody spilt out into the air and I inhaled each note. As I thought about the whirlpool of snowflakes dancing in the morning light, the silver glow of the river, and the deserted path where my footprints disappeared as quietly as they appeared, the block of ice that these memories had left in my heart began to melt.

Suddenly, the snowman stopped playing and apologised that the piece wasn't finished yet. He had learned it from the man who lived on the ground floor of the building next to the playground. The man had been writing it and practising all day but his creativity vanished midway. I thought that it must have been the owner of the Argentinian shop on the high street who occasionally gave intimate piano performances. I then remembered that I bought some empanadas from the shop earlier, so I put them in the oven to heat up.

When I brought the plate of hot empanadas to the table, the snowman's button eyes widened—

he must have been starving. Gentle steam rose from the crispy golden crust and a mouth-watering aroma filled the room. We first took a bite of the ham and cheese pastries. The smoky saltiness of the ham perfectly accompanied the mellow nutty taste of the oozy cheese. Then we tried the juicy beef empanadas filled with a mixture of tender paprika spiced beef chunks and spring onions that melted once we bit into the soft dough. The snowman looked utterly content. He asked me where the Argentinian shop was and was disappointed to find out that it was closed on Mondays. He wished that he could get some empanadas before his long trip the next day. I wondered where he was going but he just politely thanked me for the exceptional dinner and the pleasant company and said that he needed to have an early night. He left my apartment but a distant hint of the melody he had been playing on the piano lingered in the room. I walked to the window to look at the playground and he waved goodnight.

I got into bed and sleep quickly overcame me. In my dream, the snowman was walking down the dark empty high street. The full moon crept behind the clouds and its ghostly light radiated from his face. His eyes shone with determination like smouldering coals. No cars drove by and the only sound in the night was the rhythmic crunching of the snow beneath him. The snowman stopped in front of the Argentinian shop and put his hand on the brass door handle. His jelly worm finger slipped into the keyhole, and after a few seconds, a sharp click resonated in the silent street. He pushed the door open and the familiar pastry smell pulled him inside. The snowman fumbled through the shop, dimly lit by the streetlights, and walked into the kitchen at the back. He took two trays of empanadas out of the freezer and put them in the oven to bake. While he waited, he tore a few sheets of paper from the notebook on the worktop and began to write.

I woke up to the sound of police sirens piercing the night. An uneasy feeling gripped my heart and I struggled to get up and check on the snowman. My body felt listless and numb, my eyelids were heavy like lead and drowsiness quickly overwhelmed me.

The sun was shining when I opened my eyes. I replayed the events from the day before in my mind and they all seemed like a strange dream. I went to the window but the playground was empty—no sign of the snowman, just a couple of squirrels looking for food in the snow. I brewed some coffee while I skimmed through the local newspaper and I gasped at the title: "Burglary at El Gato Negro". I started reading.

"A peculiar burglary occurred at the Argentinian café, El Gato Negro, in the early hours of the morning of the 24th of January. The owner, Mr Lucas Morales, arrived for work in the morning to find the front door unlocked. He thoroughly searched the café but the only thing he discovered was missing were two trays of empanadas that had been in the freezer. No cash, documents or items of value had been touched. What he found most bizarre was the few sheets of paper left on the kitchen counter with a musical score handwritten on them that completed the piece he had been composing. Police are still investigating the incident."

I closed my eyes and imagined the snowman walking alone down the snow-covered river path that glistened in the sunlight.

His eyes sparkle victoriously as he takes a

bite of the crunchy empanada in his hand and a triumphant smile spills over his face. Somewhere, someone is playing the piano, the notes reverberate in the crisp winter air and drown in the snow.

Perfect Ghost

The first time he walks into my apartment, it's Saturday night and I am sitting on the sofa sipping a glass of chenin blanc after the delicious dinner I impressed myself with—lemon glazed salmon with sweet potatoes and red onion and parsley sauce. I am indulging in the citrusy taste of the wine when he knocks on the door. Strangely, I am not alarmed by his sudden appearance, but in the lockdown world that has turned people into shadows that you can only observe from a distance, he seems abruptly surreal. His dark blue eyes and enticing smile awaken the drowsy memory of his face that has been haunting the depths of my mind. He hugs me and my body seems to remember a lost touch, familiar and yet confusingly distant.

Spending most of my time in the tranquil world of my apartment, except for my daily runs or walks, crossing paths with the shadows of people, I haven't felt particularly lonely. My days are filled with quiet joy—the sunlight grazing the surface of my morning coffee, countless hours spent reading books, imaginary conversations with my orchid, sunset runs along the river and the enchanted forest, baking soy sauce and brown sugar chicken wings. Yet, as I hold him in my arms, something inside me stirs like an ice cube dissolving in a glass of ouzo—cold and burning at the same time, blurring my thoughts.

He takes out a bottle of red wine, pours himself a glass and sits next to me on the couch. We drink and talk about running, whiskey tastings, forgotten worlds of music festivals, meeting people before the lockdown turned people into shadows. He touches my knee through my ripped jeans and the air fills with fireflies, which flutter around our heads, little drops of gold, buzzing and whispering in our ears and diving into our glasses. I sip the wine and the sparkles slide down my throat until I am dizzy with their light. Words turn into kisses, the room spins, a cookbook falls from the kitchen counter but the air is heavy like thick clouds, and the book remains floating in front of the fridge.

Tigers in Athens

The coffee pot by the sink melts and the coffee flows towards the bottle of Monkey Shoulder.

When I wake up, he is lying next to me. In his eyes, ocean waves are crashing into each other. Sunlight floods the room and fine gold dust glitters in the air while we have coffee and avocado toast and play with the paper planes we must have made last night. He kisses me goodbye and leaves.

Slightly hungover, I wander around the apartment that now feels emptier than usual, my head in a muddle of thoughts. I try to play some music but the speaker doesn't turn on. I take the remote control to turn on the TV but the screen cracks right through the middle. Suddenly, the books on the TV stand start to fall off and the pages casually fly out. I am standing in the middle of this paper storm looking at the cracked TV screen, but all I can see is his empty mug on the coffee table. I decide to go for a run to clear my head and deal with the apartment later. I ignore the whirlpool of words that have sprung out from the books and get entangled in my hair as I tie my shoelaces and step out.

I enter the enchanted forest. The emerald

air is cool and fresh. Curious sunrays sneak in through the leaves that flap like bird wings, flakes of fluff fall from the trees in slow motion and cover the path. My steps are muffled, the white carpet swallowing the sounds. I feel lighter with each stride as I breathe in the dense perfume of the trees. It hypnotizes me and I am hovering above the white cotton candy floor. The river crawls past leisurely, its skin scintillating behind the tree trunks and the bushes jewelled with sloe berries. Miniscule bugs race each other above my eyelashes so I sometimes have to close my eyes, and the intensity of the forest penetrates my body—its raw energy trickling into my veins like tree sap. Every now and then, I pass some shadows cheerfully jogging, walking their dogs, or strolling along the beautiful spring Sunday. Someone says, "Hello," and I stop, startled, but I don't see a familiar face. I look around and a silver bottle cap drops next to me. On a tree branch, I see an elf dressed in a pink Hawaiian shirt with mint green flamingos, light blue swim shorts and yellow flip-flops. He is sipping a beer and grins at me, passing the bottle towards me. I have run about six kilometres and I feel thirsty, so I don't hesitate and take a few sips of the beer. The liquid is cold and crisp, notes of malt, pine and rain blend into what must be some magic potion. Thoughts of last night become cloudier and slowly start to dissipate among the green brilliance of the air until, eventually, the sunrays burn them to ashes that sprinkle down and vanish in the white fluff that covers the path. I thank the elf, wave goodbye and head back to my apartment.

The books have settled back in their places, all the pages neatly arranged in their usual order, and the crack on the TV screen has disappeared. I take a long shower, the events from the night before burst like soap bubbles and slide down the drain. I then try to read but I can't concentrate. The words seem to jump out of the page and linger in the air. I put the book down and stare through the window for a while. Two shadows are having a picnic in the garden across the road. A small white dog tries to steal some cheese from their blanket while they are basking in the afternoon sun.

The time inside my apartment passes sluggishly until he knocks on the door at 6:37 in the evening. His face beams when I open the door. Outside, daylight is slowly drowning in purple and pink puddles, but his presence seems to make the colours in the kitchen more vivid. The bottle of olive oil glows in fluorescent green and the red wine in our glasses dances in crimson flames. We decide to cook a lamb moussaka. He smiles at me while I slice the potatoes and my eyes water from the chopped onions. Nothing seems to exist beyond this kitchen—we are trapped in a tiny micro universe where there is just us and a hurricane of illusions in the space between the sink and the window.

We sit on the sofa and put our plates on the coffee table. As I take a bite of the moussaka and listen to his story about the swans by the river, I suddenly remember him. I have known him before... in another world without shadows. I have loved him before when we were standing on the pier, the orange sun was sinking behind the trees along the river and the golden light was spilling into the water. The boat was slowly approaching and we walked towards it, carrying our suitcases. We got on board and sat on the deck drinking Aperol Spritz and laughing. It was a perfect summer evening. Timid waves murmured below us and the breeze carried promises and the scent of wild water. But as we passed the boathouse, he suddenly kissed me, walked to the edge of the boat, and as his goodbye was still resonating in the air, he jumped in the water and turned into a silver dolphin that disappeared with the last sunrays.

But that was then. Now, he pulls me closer and the past vanishes. As I lay across his chest, time ceases to exist. I stare at the empty plates on the table while he sings the song that I like, and I wish I could stay in this moment forever.

A grumbling roar stirs the stillness and I look around to see the fibres of the carpet splitting and a crack opening in the floor. With a swift determination, it moves past my trainers by the door, along the edge of the kitchen tiles, passing my longboard, pausing for a moment in front of the radiator and continuing towards the pile of cables by the TV stand. It then crawls to the legs of the coffee table in front of us where it starts to grow bigger until the table falls into the hole by our feet. He takes my hand and jumps in. We are falling in a whirlpool of glasses, clinking joyfully, drops of red wine pirouetting on their rims, a wooden chair folding and unfolding, flying in the space by a plate of spaghetti with meatballs and tomato sauce. Swarms of books glide above our heads, navigating through a shower of strawberries, tiny jars of spices and a black and white painting of a butterfly. I hold his hand tightly and observe the objects and their movement around us without any urgency, my body feels light as a feather and I start to wonder if we are falling or floating up and if it actually makes any difference. I see the green wheels of my longboard and the elf from the enchanted forest riding it. Again, he is holding a beer in his hand. He passes the bottle towards me, and as I reach out to take it, I am pulled away. The smell of seawater floods the air, damp chillness surrounds me and the hand that I'm holding feels cold, sleek and slippery. I am on the boat again, stunned and alone staring at the shadow in the water. I let go of his hand and grab the beer bottle from the elf. I drink the potion hastily before I am submerged in water, drowning in the darkness while a rubbery tail grazes my shoulder.

When I open my eyes, I am lying on the white fluffy path in the forest. Sunlight blinds me, but as my eyes slowly adjust, I see the silhouette of a woman kneeling down and asking me if I am okay. She says she saw me trip while I was running. I look around and see groups of people—girls with coffee cups in their hands, couples walking their dogs, children shouting and chasing each other, a man lost in his thoughts, listening to his headphones. A green butterfly lands on my hand and I get up to tie my shoelaces.

Tigers in Athens

    Lia wandered around the maze of cobblestone streets in Plaka, occasionally stopping to snap a quick photo of the rows of green potted plants along the buildings and the pink and red flowers that streamed down from the rooftops like extravagant chandeliers. The late August Athenian heat dried the air that hung heavy and still. Tired of the merciless sunrays that burned her arms where her white cotton t-shirt didn't cover the skin, Lia desperately searched for a place to cool down. She scanned the little restaurants with their welcoming tables, arranged over the steps of the narrow street, and picked one at the top of the stairs, nestled in the shade below an umbrella of ivy leaves. A friendly waiter took her order, and while she waited for her food to arrive, she removed her blue sunglasses and took out a small silver mirror to wipe off the traces of smudged eyeliner under her eyes and the microscopic drops of sweat on her forehead. The trip around the Acropolis had exhausted her and she was now laughing at the prayer that she made to Athena. Why she prayed to Athena in particular, she had no idea.

Her thoughts were momentarily interrupted by the waiter, who brought out a plate of grilled octopus and courgettes, a Greek salad and a small bottle of retsina. Lia took a small bite of the octopus, drizzled with olive oil and bursting with the taste of the sea, and slowly sipped the cold drink. This was supposed to be a holiday with her boyfriend, but instead, they had separated and here she was alone, suffocating in the sweltering heat, sending prayers to the Greek gods and wishing she would meet the man of her dreams. She chuckled at the thought of how ironic it all seemed.

Flushing faintly, she focused on the man sitting at the table across from her. He wore beige loafers, white cotton trousers and a coral t-shirt and had the head of a tiger. Sensing her gaze, he looked away from his newspaper and smiled at her with an innocent, almost human smile.

Rays of sunlight desperately wove through the canopy of ivy leaves above the tables to kiss the breathtaking gold of his eyes. His face was a blend of all the colours of autumn, exquisitely streaked with black and white stripes. The immaculately trimmed hairs on top of his head occasionally shimmered like a crown of orange sapphires.

"Yia mas," he said and raised his glass of ouzo. She returned his gesture, unable to take her eyes off his. The shade of his irises changed in the light and hypnotised her. One moment, it wrapped her in its brown velvet embrace, and the next it dazzled her like amber fire that set her soul alight. The Tiger Man spoke with a soothing voice and asked her questions about her trip. She had arrived in Athens from London two days ago and was strolling along the sun-soaked streets of this ancient city on her own, eager to discover some of its secrets. They chatted for a few minutes before he said he had a meeting to go to and got up to leave.

"I would love to buy you a drink this evening if you care for some company. I will be at Balux Seaside at 8 pm," he said and gave her a charming smile.

Lia watched him walk away, disappearing around the corner behind a garland of crimson flowers that flowed down the wall of a small café. She finished her lunch and took the metro to Argyroupoli, where she had rented an apartment. After a refreshing shower, she put on a pair of snakeskin-print shorts, a black top and black leather sandals, then stepped out. Curious to explore more of the city, she decided to walk to the beach bar where she was meeting the Tiger Man but quickly regretted it.

It was supposed to be about an hour and a half walk to the beach but she felt like she had been walking for days. The relentless afternoon sun smothered her with its unbearable heat and vaporized her thoughts. She walked along an endless boulevard, breathing fumes from the innumerable cars that drove past as she tried to catch a hint of sea breeze. Not a single person walked past, there were just infinite pavements, scorched from the sun, deserted bus stops, empty petrol stations and countless inconspicuous concrete buildings. A monotonous scenery that stretched for miles. She felt utterly alone in the world. Her mind was blurry and her body felt like it didn't belong to her. She robotically put one foot in front of the other, dizzy from the high temperature, losing her sense of direction. All she could do was surrender to the blistering sun in the distance to guide her. It was now slowly turning orange and sinking down the scintillating strip of sea that she finally caught a glimpse of behind the buildings. A gentle breeze caressed her and she thought of the Tiger Man.

When she arrived at the beach bar, he was waiting for her at a table right on the sand, just a few metres away from the water. The lantern on the ground illuminated his face, which was now dark auburn with its snow-white streaks glowing against the backdrop of the deep violet sky. He was drinking whiskey and smoking shisha. The sweet aroma of wild raspberries surrounded her as she sat down and ordered an Aperol Spritz. She told him about her nightmarish journey to the beach and began to feel a little less alone. They talked about the Greek song that was playing, about the lights of the marina across the bay, about their jobs, friends and passions, about the best place to buy spanakopita and the fireworks that suddenly exploded above the sea, leaving a mesmerizing reflection in the water. But words were not necessary. Some inexplicable force beyond conversation connected them.

The Tiger Man picked up the shisha pipe and inhaled, his white whiskers slightly trembling, then blew out a cloud of smoke that engulfed Lia. The dim lights of the bar faded away along with the people, glasses of cocktails, lounge music and chattering voices. She couldn't see anything through the thick white fog. The only sound was the quiet murmur of the waves stretching their arms out to bury their fingers in the warm sand. When the smoke dispersed, there was no one around her but the Tiger Man. The tables scattered on the beach stood empty with their chairs neatly arranged and adorned with plumped-up turquoise cushions. The desolate bar was dark and silent. A starless indigo sky loomed above the sea of black water, laced with white ripples. The Tiger Man leaned over to kiss Lia and she felt light-headed from the taste of raspberries and the tingling sensation of his arms around her. With her eyes closed, she suddenly remembered her prayer to Athena. The goddess must have heard her wish. When she opened her eyes, the beach bar was full, the music was louder and the clamour of voices more animated. It was past midnight and the Tiger Man offered to drive her home.

She got in his car and they flew down the wide boulevard that had taken her to the beach. Orange street lamps flashed above them like hundreds of identical moons and green traffic lights made them drive faster. Lia felt a rush that electrified her body. The speed, the drinks at the bar, the music that flooded the car and the haunting presence of the Tiger Man were exhilarating. For a brief moment, she looked in the rear-view mirror and saw a woman sitting at the back. Her dark brown hair spilt over her shoulders like satin that reflected the headlights of the cars that passed by while her grey eyes sparkled mischievously. Her lips formed an almost imperceptible smile that was a mix of pride and amusement. Startled, Lia turned around but the back seat was empty. She looked into the mirror again but the mysterious woman was gone.

When they arrived at her apartment, the living room smelled like magnolia flowers but there were no flowers in the room or magnolia trees in the street. The lights seemed dimmer than they had been the night before. Lia had the feeling that there was someone else in the apartment but quickly abandoned the thought. She offered the Tiger Man a glass of the whiskey she had bought at the airport and played the Greek song that they heard at the beach bar. They drank the whiskey and danced on top of the marble coffee table and made love on the green leather sofa until the moon disappeared behind the white houses across the street.

Lia slept with her cheek against the soft hairs on the Tiger Man's face when she woke up from a whisper in her ear—a low female voice. She looked around but couldn't see anyone in the darkness of the room. The voice seemed to circle around her, indistinguishable but rhythmic and persistent. She got up without turning the lights on and went into the kitchen to get a glass of water. She walked out onto the balcony and strained to hear what the voice was saying.

"I have granted your wish but I will take something away from you," the voice said coldly.

"What will you take?" asked Lia, her voice dry with apprehension. But there was no reply, just the silence of the night and an owl hooting somewhere in the distance.

The next morning, she awoke from the pink sunlight that trickled into the room through the blinds. The Tiger Man was still asleep next to her. She got up and went out on the balcony. She thought about the strange voice, the image of the woman in the car, the beach bar, and the taverna where she had met the Tiger Man. She also thought about Athens but she couldn't remember anything before that. She had no recollection of her life, family, home, friends, or what she did for a living. Her memory was wiped clean. This was what Athena had taken. Panic struck her as she struggled to recall any detail that would hint at who she was. Why had she made that prayer? She bitterly regretted it now and desperately wished that she could turn back the time but there was no one to hear her wish. Tears streamed down her face as she stared breathlessly at the enormous unfamiliar city in front of her. She felt helpless and nauseous, afraid she might disappear into the void that had devoured her memories.

"Kalimera," the Tiger Man said cheerfully as he brought out a tray with cups of coffee and glasses of orange juice and set it down on the table. The sight of him irritated her at first but the warmth of his golden eyes quickly dried her tears. This was what she had wished for and it was now hers. She reached for one of the cups and caught her reflection in the polished silver tray, only to realise she now also had the head of a tiger. The Tiger Man poured milk into her coffee and asked if she wanted to go to the beach. A pair of seagulls cried above them and headed towards the sea.

The Strange Aquarium

The clock on the wall shows 1:37 am. It has been four days since our Norwegian forest cat, Toby, turned into a porcelain figurine. Damian and I are sitting in silence on the white leather sofa pondering the strange situation. Two candles in sparkly rose gold jars flicker on the table by the bottle of Malbec as we sip our wine, lost in our thoughts. As I stare at the statuette of Toby standing between our glasses, I try to recall the events that must have led to this.

Four days ago, I was in the kitchen chopping tomatoes for a pasta sauce while Toby was sitting on the marble countertop, keeping me company. He attentively observed my movements with his curious turquoise eyes and occasionally blinked with approval. Damian called me to tell me that he would be working late, so I had dinner alone and read a book. It was strange because he never worked late. When he came home past midnight, he was unusually enthusiastic and asked a lot of questions, almost as if to evade being asked anything. Some secret lurked in the air and nibbled on our trust. A hostile distance sprawled between us. When we woke up the next day, we found the porcelain statue of Toby in our bed. It looked completely identical to him as if he had been frozen in time—glassy turquoise eyes, snow-white chest and chin, shiny grey fur streaked with hints of copper brown. We kept leaving food and water in his bowls, and every morning, we found them empty.

As we sit on the sofa, I remember I filled the bowls on the kitchen floor in the morning, so I go to check. Empty. I look around the kitchen but get no clues. When I return to the living room, an aquarium has appeared in the space in front of the window and the door that leads to the balcony. It is about six inches thick and stretches from the floor all the way to the ceiling, completely sealed off from all sides. Iridescent pebbles and pearl white shells sparkle along the narrow strip of sand that covers the bottom of the tank. A dozen fiery red and dark blue fish swim peacefully among the multicolour corals and strings of seaweed that reach to the top while a single goldfish, the colour of caramelised apples, hovers in the middle, its eyes scanning the room.

Seemingly unaffected by the changes in the living room, Damian says that he wants to have a cigarette, so he takes my hand and pulls me straight through the aquarium. As we step onto the balcony, it is no longer night time. The afternoon sun caresses me with its velvet warmth as it peeks behind the trees along the river shore. We sit at the table where two mimosas wait for us and I take a sip while Damian lights his cigarette. As our glasses clink, Toby jumps on my lap. Real, fluffy, very non-porcelain Toby. He purrs softly as I stroke his grey fur that shimmers in the sunset light.

Damian smiles at me affectionately while quiet wind ruffles my hair and whispers in my ear. But as the last sunrays creep along the floor, Toby suddenly jumps from my lap onto the metal railing and plunges toward the square below the balcony. Panic grips me when Damian gets up and climbs over the railing, his eyes wild with determination, his face fearless. He drops to the ground with a thud and I run to the end of the balcony, only to catch a glimpse of him disappearing around the corner.

I decide to wait and settle back in the plastic chair that now feels rough like sandpaper. The pink and purple sky quickly turns ink blue, a moonless sky draped with scattered see-through clouds that glide like ghosts. The humid smell of the river drifts in the darkness and the relentless cold wind sends chills through my body. A terrible loneliness overwhelms me and my mind swirls in circles. Maybe they are both gone now, swept away like shattered porcelain. I could climb down the balcony as it's only one storey high, or I could try to get back into the apartment through the aquarium. Choosing the second option, I get up and stop in front of the door, the aquarium still blocking the entrance. I try to look inside the apartment but the image across the water is dark and hazy—all I can see are the luminous fish and pebbles then fog behind the glass on the other side. I take a deep breath and step forward.

For a brief moment, I am trapped inside the aquarium. My body, slightly bigger than the goldfish that circles around me, floats weightlessly in the cool water that flows through my skin. The playful flicker of the candles on the coffee table brushes the glass wall of the aquarium and faint traces of light ripple through the water. Through the billowing ribbons of seaweed, I can see Damian sitting on the sofa just like before. As he sips his red wine, the flames of the candles twinkle in the glossy pool of his dark brown eyes. Porcelain Toby sits motionless on the table. Then the glass cracks and I spill out on the ground, back to my normal size, rolling among glass, shells, blue fish and ruby pebbles that are caught in the incessant stream of water that springs from the tank.

"Are you okay?" asks Damian as he helps me up.

"Yes, but what happened to Toby?" But before he replies, I notice that the porcelain figurine is no longer on the table.

"We need to find him before the water gets too deep," says Damian as he runs to look for him behind the sofa.

The water is now up to our knees. The front panel of the aquarium is gone but the rest is still intact and a fierce waterfall pours out from the top. Dim red lights glimmer along the sides of the tank. By the time I wade to the kitchen, the water is grazing the edge of the countertops and small waves splash over the marble. There is no sign of Toby, so I go back to the living room.

"We're trapped!" shouts Damian with a worried look on his face. He tries to open the door to the hallway but the water pressure gets in the way. I frantically look around the room. The water reaches my chin and the paintings from the walls float around me like solitary rafts. Sparks from the ceiling lights shower us like a rain of silver stars, and then there is the porcelain body of Toby perched on top of the shelves along the wall opposite the aquarium. My feet are no longer touching the floor when the flood reaches Toby and drags him underwater. He sinks to the bottom and I dive towards him. I swim over the Persian rug covered with shells and colourful pebbles. Sand glistens on the wooden floorboards and I glance at the red lights of the aquarium, then at the velvet cushions floating above the white leather sofa. The goldfish skims past my head, blue and red fish surround me. I grasp Toby while Damian pulls me towards the surface.

As we float holding on to one of the paintings,

our heads almost reaching the ceiling, Damian tells me about the night he had to work late. He didn't stay in the office all evening. He drove 80 miles to a small town in the countryside. He passed the pub at the end of the high street and continued down a desolate road in the woods. Alone in the darkness with only the headlights of his car illuminating the way, his heart beat fast. The road ended in a clearing with a magnificent mansion in the middle. As he stepped out of the car, a beautiful woman with bright green eyes opened the front door of the house and led him inside. They sat by the grand fireplace in the drawing room and sipped earl grey tea while a huge ginger Maine Coon played with her three kittens on the cream carpet by their feet. The woman pointed to the kitten that Damian had bought the day before and told him that he could pick it up in two weeks. He had wanted to surprise me with a new cat called Goldfish.

There is a white flash and all the lights in our living room go off—only the blurry red lights of the aquarium still glint in the dark. Gathering all the remaining strength in our muscles, we dive towards the aquarium. We slide through the glass panel as if through a giant soap bubble and cross over to the other side.

This time, there is no balcony. We are sitting on the white sofa in the living room—no raging water, broken glass or shells, fish or aquarium around. Silhouettes cast by the candles on the table swim in our glasses of red wine. Toby is sleeping curled up on my lap, his body perfectly soft and warm, while Damian shows me the photo of the orange Maine Coon kitten called Goldfish.

Fog

The fog appeared early on Monday morning. The fiery November colours had faded overnight. Leaves like dried clementine peels hung on the branches of trees and a torn rug—a patchwork of pale yellow and mousy brown rags—covered the sidewalks. Wisps of mist, fine as spider webs, enveloped the houses. I had run out of oat milk for my morning coffee, so I walked towards the store to buy a carton, but an uneasy feeling followed me along the street. The local café flickered at the end of the road and I decided to go there instead, enticed by the warm glow of the green lamps on the tables. I went inside, greeted by the robust scent of freshly brewed coffee, and hurriedly closed the door behind me, afraid to let the fog inside. I ordered an oat flat white and a croissant and settled in the burgundy armchair in the corner by the window.

I felt as if someone was watching me through the window but the street was empty... only the fog was lurking outside, smothering the crumpled leaves on the pavement with its ghostly veil. I sipped my coffee slowly, reluctant to leave the cosy café. The outlines of the houses across the street gradually vanished until the buildings looked like they had been submerged in a pool of mist that slowly nibbled on them and, eventually, devoured them.

When I went back outside, a thick milky white layer of fog that reached up to my knees covered the road. I couldn't see my feet or where the sidewalk ended. As I waddled in this river of cloud, I could feel the fog slithering around my legs, tugging at my jeans. I wanted to run home but it kept pulling me with its tentacles, so I made slow progress. The street was deserted—only a red car silently floated away and faded in the distance. It was unnervingly quiet. There was just the muffled sound of the slippery piles of leaves being flattened by my leather boots.

After what felt like an eternity, I finally reached the front door of my building and stumbled inside. I ran up the stairs to my apartment on the third floor as fast as I could, not once looking back. I needed something to distract myself with, so I took an orange from the fridge, sat on the white fur rug in the living room and started slowly peeling it on the blue porcelain plate on top of the coffee table. Why had I felt so scared earlier? It seemed silly now in the comfort of my living room since it was just fog, ordinary November fog. But as I ate the orange segments, the room seemed to get lighter.

I looked at the window and all I could see from the floor was a white background—a blank page where the contours of the tall block of flats opposite my building had been erased. I stood up to have a closer look and I froze. An ocean of fog had engulfed the street, the cars, the red brick houses and even the trees that soared higher than the window. It was as if the house had risen up in the sky and floated among impenetrable white clouds. Infinite whiteness.

I turned on the TV to check the news but all the channels displayed a white background. Getting more anxious, I tried to call my friends but there was no signal. What was happening? I felt utterly alone, as if I was locked in a waterproof container at the bottom of the ocean. Except that it wasn't waterproof.

Thin lines of mist were creeping in under the door and through the keyhole like fine smoke. I quickly covered the gap under the door with a towel but the fog sneaked in effortlessly. Within minutes, the air in the living room was hazier. Sheer white waves licked the surfaces of the grey couch, the plush cushions, and the glass coffee table with the porcelain plate full of orange peels. They crawled up and down the walls and above the wooden floors and curled up on the fur rug. There was nothing I could do to stop this invasion. I went to the kitchen at the end of the room, took the bottle of Monkey Shoulder, dusted it off the clouds that rolled over the marble countertops, and poured myself a glass. Neat. There was no use for ice in the middle of this disaster.

I sat on the couch, put my feet up on the armrest and just watched things unfold as I sipped my whiskey. The fog was getting denser now. I could barely make out the titles of the books on the shelf below the TV. After a while, I couldn't see the bottles of olive oil and balsamic vinegar on the kitchen counter at the far end of the room or the sink... until, eventually, the whole kitchen disappeared behind a veil of whiteness—cupboards, tiles and even the silver fridge. The whiskey warmed me and gave me a sort of reassurance. I held the glass in my hand now because the sea of fog had swallowed the coffee table along with the blue plate and orange peels. I couldn't even see my arms at this point, I just sipped the whiskey wrapped in this boundless cloak of fog. The taste of whiskey mixed with the chilled taste of vapour made me think of wet pavements and grey skies.

Entirely surrounded by the fog and unable to see anything other than a thick white cloud, I closed my eyes. The faint smell of autumn rain and decomposing leaves filled my nostrils. Humid air blew like pleasant wind that gently caressed my face. The fog felt like a friend now, familiar, close. He had settled comfortably on the couch next to me and embraced me in his cold arms. It was a calm coldness, one that sharpened your senses and cleared your mind.

In this blindness, with my eyes closed, I could see the sea, silver and tranquil, resting peacefully below the grey Piraeus sky. A group of curious sunrays managed to slip through the clouds and dipped into the water. The ripples they made shimmered like diamonds, scattered across the surface of the sea. I kept looking for you in the brightness of those diamonds and in the crystals of cold ouzo that complimented the luscious taste of grilled octopus... in the salty breeze that snuck into the taverna and blended with the smell of fried calamari... in the golden drops of olive oil that bejewelled the paper tablecloth. I was trying to find you behind the cigarette smoke in crowded clubs and in the sunrises that burned my eyes as I left them... in the feather-soft pillows smudged with my mascara... in a stylish hotel room, in the scent of the luxurious body lotion in miniature bottles that were immaculately arranged on the concrete bathroom sink... on rooftops, adorned with an endless ceiling of stars, and in glasses of Malagouzia. But you had irrevocably vanished.

We had been so happy in the Athenian August afternoon heat as we sat on our sun-drenched balcony and watched the ships sail towards the port of Piraeus. We sipped very sweet Greek coffee in pale green porcelain cups. I wore a long dress made of white lace, which the wind played with, and you had black sunglasses on. The smell of fried courgettes wafted from the neighbour's open window along with the occasional barking of their dog. You made a joke that wasn't very funny but I was high on sugar and caffeine, so I laughed hysterically. Out of the corner of my eye, the perspective seemed somewhat distorted, as if you had moved further away. I looked at you and you were sitting in the same chair as before but you were reduced in size. You kept talking as if nothing unusual was happening but you gradually kept shrinking.

Unable to react, I just watched you become smaller and smaller, shorter than the porcelain coffee cup on the table in front of you until, eventually, you completely disappeared and all I could see was the yellow cushion on the chair where you had been sitting. In the distance, "Roza" by Dimitris Mitropanos was playing.

I opened my eyes to see if the fog was still there and the dazzling whiteness pierced my eyes. I squinted until my pupils adjusted to the light and I blinked slowly, hoping to distinguish some shape or colour in the room but it was to no avail. I wondered what time it was... it felt like hours had passed since I came back to the apartment, but for all I knew, it could have been a few minutes. My body was beginning to feel numb under the growing weight of the cloud that kept getting denser and denser, and slowly replaced the air in the room. I was breathing fog now. It filled my lungs with the raw taste of earth and rotting leaves and rain, soaking through my skin and into my bones. I lay there motionless and started to feel sleepy. The whiskey glass tumbled out of my hand and landed with a dull thud on what must have been the rug.

I began to imagine that I would turn into vapour and how every cell of my body would be transformed into mist—from my toes to my hair follicles. The continuously expanding fog would push the window open and I would slide outside, only to realise that the air had cleared. I would watch the bright red London buses as I soared freely above them. I would fly above the Thames, perhaps all the way to Piraeus. I would land on our old balcony, hoping to find you in the parallel universe that had absorbed you. And you would be there with your black sunglasses on, sipping Greek coffee out of a green cup. You would look at me — an ethereal cloud, tinted pink from the sun that sank in the indigo-blue Aegean sea.

I woke up on the couch from the sound of the door opening. The fog had dissipated and only small puddles of mist lingered above the floor. I saw your silhouette in the doorway with the late afternoon sunlight streaming behind and it felt like the Piraeus summer flooded my London apartment. I could almost hear "Roza" playing somewhere in the background.

The Run

The harsh Sunday morning sunlight pulls the sheets away from me and I wake up to a clear blue sky. It looks as if it has been photoshopped—a vibrant fake sky ready to burst into the room through the windows. The dark wooden beams on the ceiling hover above me and the air is chilly. I arrived at the cottage last night in an attempt to escape from my thoughts of a past love who has left only ashes in my heart... but it seems they might have followed me.

When I finally force myself to get up, I go to the kitchen to make some coffee and peanut butter toast. Microscopic specks of dust flutter around the room, illuminated by the sunrays. Outside, the sun spills its October light all over the mountain. It looks like a good day for a run. I put on my jogging clothes and trainers and head out.

The fresh scent of pine trees and fallen autumn leaves, drying from the morning dew, blends into an invigorating perfume that fills my lungs. I inhale deeply and start running along the trail that leads to a clearing, where a few cottages are scattered. An old man is arranging the plastic chairs on a porch, while a woman next to him puts a plate of pancakes and blueberry jam on the table. A curious grey dog follows me for a while but then loses interest and heads back. I jog past the small café that only sells two types of chocolate biscuits, an unpopular brand of crisps, Coke and beer. The familiarity of the scenery gives me a distant hint of a forgotten warm feeling of joy—a feeling that has been buried beneath the solitude of my heart.

I enter the woods, and as I descend the trail, the world starts rolling around me in waves the colour of copper and pomegranate seeds. An intense silence surrounds me, disturbed only by melancholic bird songs and the sound of twigs crunching beneath my feet. Complete stillness permeates the air and as I glide downhill, I suddenly think of the place where I met him—the cat gallery.

It was a quirky shop by the river where you could buy or simply admire various pieces of art or everyday objects inspired by cats. Paintings of cats covered the walls and cat-shaped salt and pepper shakers, plant pots and mugs filled the shelves. A large blue sofa and a couple of cosy green armchairs by the window invited you to unwind comfortably with one of the cat-themed books. I was skimming through a book called "The Cat Chronicles" when he sat down next to me on the sofa and asked if I liked the shop. It turned out he was the owner. We chatted for a while over cups of chai tea latte and ginger biscuits. Our conversation flowed from descriptions of the cats we used to have as teenagers to passionate discussions of our favourite books and the power of healing crystals. There was a special light in his dark brown eyes—one that drew me in irrevocably, so when he asked me if I wanted to go for dinner sometime, naturally I agreed.

Our endless sunset walks along the river, countless midnight wine and cheese dates, lazy Saturday mornings in bed laughing for hours, and candlelit dinners at our local steak restaurant all seem like moments from another life now. It all happened in a universe so volatile, I blinked and it evaporated. Now all that exists is this mountain, as infinite and lonely as the emptiness inside me. I keep running, and the further I run, the denser the forest becomes. The red of the leaves gets deeper, the orange darker.

I hear a sudden rustling in the bush to my right and a golden fox leaps out and lands on the trail a few meters in front of me. Startled, I stop and stare at it. Her fur shimmers in the sunlight like stardust as she looks at me with her deep charcoal eyes. As I stand there hypnotized, I feel like something has shifted in the air—a glimmer of hope has emerged from the darkness that has cloaked my heart for the past few months. While I am still in a state of trance, the fox turns around and starts running along the trail. Without hesitation, I start running after her. We cruise downhill, stepping over tree roots that have crawled onto the path and rocks that roll beneath us. Instead of trying to escape, the fox seems to be guiding me, going at a steady pace and occasionally stopping to make sure I am following.

We reach a meadow with a stream in the middle, where the fox stops to drink. I fill my

Tigers in Athens

water bottle and take a few sips. The water is cold and refreshing. After our quick rest, we cross the meadow and the trail continues uphill. The steep incline intimidates me. While the fox leisurely jogs forward, I struggle to keep up. My muscles begin to strain and beads of sweat roll down my forehead. Trees weave their branches like thick spiderwebs above us, blocking the sunlight until I can't see the sky. In the heavy shadow that weighs me down, the fox glitters in front of me like a firefly, leading my way. My mind gets cloudy.

I think about the last time I walked past the cat gallery. I peered inside through the windows at the vast emptiness that had comfortably settled in, erasing all traces of the cat world. The hay-coloured wooden floors stretched infinitely. There were no longer any colourful paintings and posters on the white walls that now stood silently with a blank stare. Without the numerous shelves overflowing with cat-themed objects, the space looked enormous. The bright sunlight that streamed through the windows exposed this new vacant reality even more. Along with the comfortable blue sofa, the volumes of books filled with cat stories, the cushions, aprons and duvet covers with cat prints and the enchanting atmosphere of the shop... he was also gone. He just vanished without a trace or an explanation.

Raindrops begin to fall down my cheeks. Cold and smooth, they try to wipe off the remnants of sadness on my skin. They fall and fall, drenching my blue leggings and pink top, but the heavier and more tired I feel, the more determined I am to follow the fox.

An ominous grey sky looms above us, sending thunder and lightning. The vibrant colours of the trees have been washed out and the air is thick and clingy. My legs feel like concrete and I am out of breath. Dizziness overwhelms me. I am running in a whirlpool of raging clouds. I trip over piles of brown leaves scattered along the trail, and in the middle, the fox is calling me with her quiet black eyes. A blinding stream of light flashes and my foot gets caught in a tree root that has gripped the path. I lose my balance and fall down.

I wake up lying on the ground. The rain has stopped and the air is filled with the raw smell of drying earth. The sun is shining through the emerald-green pine trees that glisten in the light. I look around but there is no trace of the fox. I get up, and as I take a step forward, I begin to feel lighter as if I have just woken up from a bad dream. But something seems off. I look around and then down at my feet, only to realise they have turned into golden paws that shimmer on top of my blue leggings crumpled on the path.

I reach the end of the trail and go to the edge of the cliff. The sun is slowly disappearing behind the dark silhouettes of trees and embraces the mountain in its crimson arms. An orange and pink cape drapes the sky. As I sit still, sparkling in the amber sunset light, the last fiery sunrays get entangled in my golden fur and sprinkle dust of joy in my heart—joy as vast as the burning horizon ahead and as limitless as the possibilities that emerge from darkness.

Rose Gold

A delicate poppy cautiously peeked out of the damp earth by the trunk of an ancient oak tree and slowly emerged from the ground, looking around with curiosity. The tree welcomed her to the forest and ceremonially introduced her to the inhabitants. Magnificent sycamores and ash trees bowed gracefully, followed by waist-high nettles and thistles. A boisterous ant colony greeted the flower with loud cheers and local gossip that left her bewildered, then came buzzing bees who whispered secrets to her, accompanied by interminable celebratory bird songs, the flapping of wings and the vigorous shaking of fluttering leaves and clumsy branches. The day rolled in one exuberant mass of the cries of blue kingfishers, the dances of shiny green beetles scuttling around, the breathtaking acrobatics of fearless squirrels that defied gravity, and in the centre of all this chaotic performance, Poppy stood shy and quietly marvelled at the motion of the new world that surrounded her.

Evening approached and the patch of ground around the oak tree that had been in permanent shade suddenly grew lighter as sunrays crept in through the blossoming blackthorn shrubs. They looked like golden gods, grinning assertively as they warmed everything they touched with their immortal hands. Poppy watched them with awe and her gaze settled on the sunray that was a slightly different shade from the rest—a subtle rose gold. He was the most beautiful thing she had seen all day, a colour so mesmerizing, it made everything else look dull and worn out. He noticed her and approached her with interest.

"Good afternoon, I'm Rose Gold," his voice flowed like thick honey, luscious and smooth. Even though he had seen many poppies, something struck him about the vibrancy of this fragile flower. She reminded him of the fiery feathers of the birds of paradise he had seen earlier. He told Poppy about the odd-looking birds that he had found so captivating. Their wings were the burning colour of the setting sun, their heads, dyed half bright yellow and half sleek dark green, their velvety crimson chests and the long tail that split in two and looked more like soft hair than feathers, fading from yellow to snow-white. With her limited knowledge of the world, Poppy struggled to imagine what those birds would look like, so he made comparisons with the colours, shapes and textures from the small piece of forest that she knew. Utterly enthralled, she listened to his stories about faraway places and wished she could follow him on his journey. How nice it would be to soar like the birds of paradise.

After a while, the sunrays began to withdraw and Rose Gold told Poppy that it was time for him to go and that he would be back tomorrow. The golden light dissipated and dusk spilt around the flower. As the darkness deepened, she thought about the hospitality of her new neighbours, the songs of the robins and woodpigeons who had sung their hearts out, the cosy shelter of the old oak tree, but mostly, she thought about Rose Gold and the way he had gilded the air with his presence, about the limitless world that belonged to him.

Morning came and the forest creatures and

plants began to awake. A lime green caterpillar slithered past Poppy and playfully shook her out of her sleep. Having settled comfortably in her new environment, the flower joked with the ants, sang with the sparrows and laughed with the bluebells across the path. Living was easy and carefree. The sun shone somewhere beyond the trees and only a vague imprint of its light filtered through the thick tree crowns. Greenness and tranquillity permeated the air, but as the hours passed, Poppy became impatient and aloof. When would Rose Gold return? She was staring disinterestedly at a little ivory rock in front of her when a warm wave of sunshine flooded in and she saw him next to her. This time, he told her stories about eternally snow-covered mountain peaks that rose above the clouds, airplanes, people tanning on a beach, sunflowers, buildings of stone and concrete that reached the sky and tortoiseshell cats that stretched in the sun.

And so, this sequence continued. Poppy would spend the day half-heartedly participating in conversations, becoming more and more detached from the bustling world around her, impatiently waiting for the afternoon when Rose

Gold would visit her. At night, she would dream of him. Weeks passed in that manner until, one day, she woke up to cool drops of rain. The leaves of the trees and blades of grass glistened in the emerald half-light of the forest. The soothing sound of the rain had replaced the bird songs. At first, Poppy enjoyed the calm drizzle and the sudden transformation of her surroundings, but as the hours rolled by, she grew uneasy and restless. Surely by now Rose Gold should be here, she thought, gazing in the direction of the blackthorn bush. But the light never changed and neither he nor the other sunrays appeared.

Night fell and Poppy began to tremble in the fine dust of rain that the trees sifted through their intertwined branches. In the empty silence, she longed for the warm touch of Rose Gold and visualized the stories he had told her. They seemed so distant and strange now, even though only a day had passed. "He will be back tomorrow," she reassured herself before falling into a delirious slumber. She dreamt that she was flying on the wings of one of the birds of paradise that Rose Gold had described to her. The bird gracefully navigated among the trees towards a chunk of light pink sky. As they lifted above the forest, dazzling brightness engulfed them, and while Poppy struggled to make sense of the scenery, Rose Gold landed softly on the silky feathers of the bird.

The next few days were the same—intermittent raindrops, dusk that lasted until night time and fog that seeped through the trees. Poppy felt weak and tired, dozing on and off, dreaming vivid dreams until she no longer knew if she was awake or asleep. The ants brought her special nectars, the birds sang to her, a yellow butterfly embraced her, but nothing could revive her. Her once radiant red petals were now washed out, drooping listlessly from the frail stem that swayed lightly from side to side. Nothing interested her until, one day, a brightly coloured object got entangled in the branches of the oak tree and caught her attention.

"Abigail! Be careful not to fall, darling," a voice called in the distance and a little girl ran along the path that passed the oak tree. Her blonde hair was tied up in two glossy pigtails, she wore a white t-shirt, ripped jeans and red trainers and her blue eyes scanned the crowns of the trees.

"I see it, Daddy!" she exclaimed and started climbing the oak tree without hesitation. Still dazed, Poppy watched the agile girl go swiftly up, branch by branch, until she reached the object and took it down. A kite. Abigail had been walking around the clearing at the end of the forest with her dad when she saw the kite roaming the grey sky on its own, wild and free as the bird of paradise printed on it. Then, either the direction of the wind changed or the kite simply decided to land and headed towards the trees.

Walking back towards the clearing, Abigail carefully examined the kite. Once she was out of the forest, she tried to fly it but the kite wouldn't obey. Time after time she threw it towards the sullen clouds but it always plummeted to the ground. Tears of exasperation ran down Abigail's cheeks until, eventually, her dad convinced her to go home and try again tomorrow.

That night, she had a dream about the bird painted on the kite. With her flame-red wings spread out, the bird soared high and drew invisible paintings in the air. Her long tail billowed lightly in the wind like weightless strands of gold. In her beak, the bird held a small red flower. Bird and flower glided together above fields of sunflowers, snow peaks, sandy beaches, beneath airplanes and over concrete blocks of flats with tortoiseshell cats sleeping on the balconies.

When she woke up the next day, Abigail had a plan. Sitting at the kitchen table by the window, she reluctantly chewed her peanut butter and banana toast and looked at the forest in the distance. A colourless sky hung above the trees as people in wellies and beige jumpers walked their dogs in the clearing. The grass was the faded colour of wheat, burned from the summer sun that hid somewhere behind the thick clouds. After she finished her breakfast, Abigail put on a yellow waterproof jacket and her trainers, took the kite and a roll of tape, then ran outside.

Under the oak tree, Poppy stood wistfully, her shrunken petals quivering in the wind. As she walked along the path, Abigail noticed the grief-stricken flower and kneeled down to inspect it. The once bright red poppy looked so feeble and unhappy that it wouldn't survive another day. Abigail plucked her gently from the ground. The thin stem snapped unresistingly, leaving the flower to the mercy of the little girl's hands. Abigail held the kite and carefully taped the poppy to the red feathers painted on the nylon fabric. Then she stood up and started running down the green tunnel formed by the crowns of the trees along the path, kicking pieces of gravel with her red trainers. The circle of white light in the distance grew bigger and bigger and she was out on the clearing. Her fingers began to sweat and her heart beat faster. She took a deep breath and released the kite into the air.

Time stopped as the kite glided forward in a straight line, the red feathers of the bird of paradise looking heavy and tired, and just as it slowed down, forlorn and about to drop, the wind caught it and raised it up. Abigail watched it fly up, shrinking in the dove grey sky and wildly pulling the strings in her hands until they tore and it continued its flight unbridled. She followed its journey with a smile of satisfaction shimmering on her face and thought about the little flower cruising in the sky and the views it would have never seen.

Poppy woke up from one of her recurrent dreams, only to find herself inside the dream. Lying on top of the wings of the bird of paradise she had seen so many times in her sleep, she soared above a river, shining silver below the darkening sky. The kite moved smoothly in and out of ragged clouds. Shrunken and fading away, Poppy gathered her last remaining strength to take in the breathtaking views until the tape that held her to the kite came loose and she drifted away, weightless in the wind. As she floated through a scattered mist of clouds, sunlight suddenly streamed in. Golden, dazzling, timeless sunlight. And Rose Gold, self-assured and bursting with life.

Life briefly trickled back into Poppy's body at the sight of him and her dried-up petals flushed with colour. Once again, she was ecstatic as she danced in a pool of golden light, high above the glittering river and the viridian waves of trees that covered the riverbanks. She wanted to call out to him. She had so many things to say... so many questions to ask, but her energy was abandoning her.

The wind was quietly dying down and Poppy slowly began to descend towards the water that looked like a crumpled sheet of gold foil. Rose Gold finally saw her and, smiling his most dazzling smile, he caught her in his arms. A drape of pink air enveloped her.

From the bridge that crossed the river, Abigail watched the burning sunset and searched the orange sky for the kite, wondering if it was still nearby or if it had travelled miles away. Somewhere where the sky touched the water, she thought she caught a glimpse of a red flower following the last sunrays as they moved in the direction that the sun was slowly sinking beyond the river and colouring the water rose gold.

Kali Orexi

The pot on the stove bubbled quietly as the mouth-watering aroma of succulent chicken, oregano and sweet onions, melting in a tomato sauce, filled the kitchen. The glass lid was slightly open and steam gently rose up. Through the steam, a miniature hand appeared and gripped the edge of the pot, followed by another hand, and a tiny head emerged from the stew. A man, no taller than five centimetres, dressed in a white suit, climbed up and sat on the rim of the pot, scanning the kitchen with his shiny black eyes that kept blinking as if trying to adjust to the light. He jumped onto the kitchen counter and the tomato sauce residue slid off his suit, leaving it impeccably white.

In the dining room, Maria was setting the table to the sound of relaxing jazz music—two blue plates, white linen napkins and silver cutlery that glistened as the pillar candles flickered. Maria's deep brown eyes glistened too with a flame of excitement and anticipation as she placed a small bowl of plump green olives and cubes of goat's cheese by the basket of bread. Her straight brown hair shone with auburn hues every time it caught the light from the candles. She wore a black dress with large white polka dots and red lipstick. She looked at her watch—fifteen minutes until her client arrived. She went into the kitchen to check on the food.

The delicious smell of the chicken and okra stew gave her a sense of confidence as she turned off the heat. She poured half of the stew into a large white ceramic bowl painted with blue flowers and carried it to the dining room table, followed by a couple of crystal glasses and a bottle of South African merlot. She carefully placed a bunch of fresh flowers in the pale pink vase on the table. The arrangement of the table was immaculate. There was just the final detail missing. She clapped her hands twice and Andreas, the little man, appeared from behind the saltshaker and bowed. The doorbell rang.

Maria hurried towards the front door, briefly

stopping in front of the mirror in the hallway to check her appearance and nodded to herself with approval. She opened the door and greeted her client with a welcoming smile and sincere warmth in her voice as she did every time. Kostas, a man in his mid-forties with dark brown hair speckled with tiny flecks of white and sullen eyes that betrayed his sadness, stood hesitantly in the doorway. Maria took his black coat and led him to the dining room. At the sight of the beautifully decorated table in the dimly lit room and lured by the enticing smell of the food, he seemed to relax. He settled in one of the chairs as Maria poured him a glass of wine, and he began telling her his story.

Kostas had been married to his wife for three years, living happily with her in a large apartment on the fifth floor of a white villa in Glyfada. From the roof terrace that wrapped around the apartment, they used to watch the mesmerizing sunsets over the Aegean sea, sipping coffees or wine and discussing daily events, art, work or where to go for dinner. One night, he had been awoken by a knock on the bedroom window. He looked around the room, illuminated solely by the whispers of light from the stars dotting the summer sky, only to discover the empty space beside him. He thought that his wife might have somehow locked herself out on the roof terrace, so he went outside to check. In the humid silence of the August night, he heard a low tapping noise. Tap, tap, tap. Did he imagine that it was the sound of his wife's heels? He walked around the apartment to the other side of the terrace where the big glass table stood surrounded by the neatly arranged wooden chairs covered with white cushions. Then he saw her. A magpie with glossy black feathers that reflected the moonlight paced around the surface of the table impatiently. At the sight of him, she stood still and stared into his eyes. This lasted for what felt like an eternity... it was as if the bird longed to convey a message but hesitated, unable to find the right words. In the end, she spread her black cloak of wings and disappeared into the darkness of the night. All that remained on top of the table was something that he hadn't noticed before, something that glistened as the moon watched over—his wife's satin nightgown.

The police searched the apartment countless

times looking for clues, but it seemed like she had vanished into thin air. This happened a year ago. Kostas didn't dismiss the possibility that his wife had been transformed into a magpie, even though it seemed senseless and illogical. But he was certain that she would not return and was desperate to erase the pain from her absence. This is why he had come to Maria's house.

Maria didn't advertise her business but people always found her. Her clients rarely returned, and if they did, it was for a different matter. One session was enough to free them from their heartache and it all started with her magically tasting food.

The man took a bite of the juicy chicken, caressed by the luscious sauce of ripe sun-kissed tomatoes and fragranced with the freshness of thyme. He slowly sipped the wine. The comforting warmth of the dish and the simple but quality ingredients that blended into a symphony of flavours soothed him and he felt his pain subdue. Then, Andreas, who was hiding behind a book on the bookshelf behind the table, began to sing.

He sang a zeibekiko song. His deep voice flooded the room with low notes of melancholy and poetry that spilt out of his lungs like tidal waves devouring sand castles on an empty beach. He sang about a lost love with unforced sadness, the lyrics materialising as the feelings that Kostas was experiencing. The song meandered between the wine glasses and blue plates and settled inside Kostas's heart, absorbing his pain. When the last note stopped resonating in the room, Kostas felt free from his heartache. This was how Maria's clients were healed. Through his singing, Andreas carefully extracted the feelings that caused them pain and left them to dissipate at the bottom of their wine glasses. The clients never saw him, assuming it was a recording that Maria played for them.

After Kostas left, in a trance-like state and with an expression of deep relief and lightness on his face, Maria started clearing the plates. Andreas was sitting on top of one of the wine glasses as she carried them into the kitchen.

"Thank you for tonight," she said with a sweet smile on her face. He just nodded silently. He rarely spoke—it was as if he wanted to preserve his voice for singing. He waved goodbye and jumped from the wine glass, diving into the pot with the remaining stew on the kitchen counter, and disappeared. Maria was left alone with her thoughts.

She remembered the first time Andreas appeared. She had always been a good cook, but after her last relationship left her heartbroken, it seemed to her that her dishes acquired a more special taste. It was as if the leftover love that she still had blended with the food.

One evening, as the last sunset rays danced along the kitchen counter, flirting with the purple orchid by the cookbooks, Maria was stirring a pot of fava, lost in a moment of sadness when Andreas sprung out of the yellow peas and landed on top of the black pepper grinder. Before she had time to react, he began to sing. Hypnotised by his song, she stirred the fava mechanically and watched the sunrays on the wooden counter crawl back towards the window. When dusk fell and tinted the kitchen with a bluish hue, Andreas stopped singing, said goodnight politely and plunged into the pot. Maria carefully stirred the peas but there was no trace of him. She served some of the fava on a green plate, adding a drizzle of olive oil and a squeeze of lemon juice, and carried it to the dining room along with some pita bread and a small glass of white wine.

She tasted the food and sipped the wine, wondering why she felt differently as the singing of Andreas still echoed in her head. Had she altered the fava recipe somehow? Or was it the wine that tasted strange? It was only when her residual feelings of sorrow didn't reappear that she realised what the change was.

The evening following the dinner with Kostas brought the beautiful Eleni to Maria's house. She was a writer in her thirties who had lost her inspiration for writing after the separation from her last boyfriend a few months ago.

When she walked into the dining room, Andreas, who was leaning on the vase with sunflowers on the table by the window, was dazzled. He squinted, blinded by the light that Eleni seemed to radiate in the room. Her hair was the colour of beach sand at sunset, glossy and golden, flowing like honey over her shoulders. Her eyes had stolen fragments of a clear blue sky—the kind that appears after a summer storm, full of promise and hope. A veil of sadness covered her delicate face, but with every bite of the shrimp saganaki that Maria had prepared, the veil grew thinner and more transparent. Andreas sang like never before. The emotion in his voice was palpable. The words rolled off his tongue and lightly touched Eleni's arms like butterfly wings.

When the last song ended and Eleni was finishing a piece of chocolate and orange cake, her eyes smiling as she wiped her chocolate-covered lips with a napkin, Andreas felt that he needed to see her again. But how could he, a 5cm tall man, who only existed when Maria cooked, ever be a part of her life? He barely had time to dwell on the question when he was presented with an opportunity that he didn't hesitate to take.

"The cake was delicious! Could I have one more slice to take home? It would be great with my coffee tomorrow morning," Eleni asked with excitement in her voice.

"Yes, of course," Maria replied and ran into the kitchen as Andreas held onto the sleeve of her dress and floated unnoticed beside her. She cut a big slice of the cake and looked in the cupboard for a plastic container to put it in.

Andreas decided to take his chance and jumped into one of the soft chocolate cream roses decorating the slice. Maria placed the cake in the plastic box and carried it to the living room.

After Eleni left, Maria was surprised not to find Andreas but she assumed that he had already gone back to the food that he came out of.

The next morning when Eleni woke up and walked into the kitchen to make a coffee, she couldn't believe her eyes. The lid of the cake box was lying on the floor and a deep purple orchid had sprung out of the cake. Was it Maria who had planted it? But how would it grow overnight? Eleni wondered for a few moments but she felt so happy after her emotional transformation from the previous night and decided to take it as a sign of a new beginning. She took the orchid out of the cake, carefully washed it and placed it in a silver pot by the window in her living room.

Sunlight bathed the room and the large grey armchair where Eleni was sitting and sipping her coffee. From where she was, it almost seemed to her that there was a halo above the orchid and, indeed, what a magnificently angelic flower it was. There was something different about it but she couldn't figure out exactly what it was. It was as if it changed colour. When she had seen it the first time, it looked purple, but now it was a vibrant red. She marvelled at it, smiling. Andreas smiled too from his orchid body—so profound was his happiness that it turned the flowers fiery red.

In the evening, when Andreas failed to appear from the tray of colourful stuffed peppers, Maria panicked. Konstantina, the lady who lived on the fifth floor, was coming for dinner. She was in her eighties and had recently lost her husband. Maria thought about cancelling but felt sorry for her elderly neighbour and decided to go through with the dinner.

Peppers stuffed with rice, herbs and raisins, freshly baked olive bread and a crisp green salad with pomegranate seeds and graviera cheese lay on the table when Konstantina arrived. Soothing jazz music played as the two women shared stories along with the delicious food and a carafe of retsina. Konstantina's brown eyes glowed with delight in the warm atmosphere of Maria's apartment. It seemed to Maria that even without Andreas, the evening had been successful when her neighbour thanked her a dozen times for the hospitality and the wonderful evening and left with a smile on her face.

After Konstantina was gone, Maria lay down on the green couch in the living room, her head sinking comfortably into the plush burgundy cushion. She thought about her past clients and the broken hearts that she had mended with the help of Andreas. Had he really existed? Had her clients really been healed from their heartache or had it all been in her imagination? Her head was spinning from the retsina and no answers came. She closed her eyes and imagined Andreas singing in a different dining room, the candles flickering and flowers decorating the table. She fell into a blissful sleep and dreamt about orchids—purple and red.

The lights were off in Eleni's apartment. Only the green lamp on her desk illuminated her face as she wrote in a notebook, occasionally glancing at her orchid. She was writing a story about an orchid who had a magical singing voice. Her creative inspiration had returned along with her good mood and she giggled in her head at the odd stories she imagined. Andreas watched her from the silver pot, singing silently in his mind.

In Glyfada, Kostas sat on his roof terrace and sipped a whiskey, looking at the white and red webs of light that the cars, buzzing along the boulevard in front of him, wove. Behind was the sea, glossy like black satin, sparkly like diamonds shining in the moonlight. He felt hopeful, as if everything was possible in the world. He took another sip of the whiskey and closed his eyes, deeply inhaling the sea breeze. It was salty but with a hint of something sweet... a familiar perfume. He opened his eyes and saw the black magpie on the chair beside him.

Land of Gods

The white rabbit raced down the hotel corridor, gliding along the polished marble floors. I ran behind him, trying to keep up with his incredible speed. He occasionally glanced back at me with his ruby eyes as if to check if I was still following. The corridor seemed endless. I could have sworn that there were no more than ten rooms on this floor when I arrived, but now it looked like there were hundreds. The rabbit ran and ran, illuminating the black velvet wallpapered walls in the distance.

Suddenly, all the lights went off. I stood in the darkness with only the sound of my beating heart. A few moments later, when the lights came back on, I found myself in front of a lift. The silver doors opened and a human-sized rabbit dressed in a maid's uniform came out of the lift with a tray of neatly folded towels.

I woke up sweating. The hotel room was dark and I felt an emptiness that hadn't been there earlier. I frantically turned the bedside light on and looked towards the end of the bed. The cage on the floor was empty. I checked under the bed and around the room, but the rabbit was nowhere to be seen. Was it another dream? I kept closing and opening my eyes, but every time I opened them, I ended up in the same hotel room with an empty cage and no rabbit. Then I noticed something at the bottom of the cage—a white envelope. I opened it with trembling hands and began to read.

"Your bunny is safe. But as an early Christmas present, I have decided to make your trip more exciting by giving you a challenge to complete to get the rabbit back. There is a Christmas tree at Ilias' Taverna in Piraeus. On top of the tree is an ornament that you must collect. It won't be easy, but don't worry, Dionysus will help you.

Athena"

I laughed. What kind of a joke was this? My first thought was that Anastasia had conspired with the hotel staff, but it didn't really sound

Tigers in Athens

like her. Anastasia was my friend and the reason for my trip. She had recently moved to London with her husband, and now that she was eight months pregnant, she suddenly missed her pet rabbit, which she had left at her grandmother's house in Piraeus. Anastasia desperately wanted to be reunited with her pet for Christmas, and as she couldn't fly and needed her husband in London, she asked me to go to Athens and bring the rabbit. She would take care of all the expenses surrounding the trip.

I travelled to Athens very often since I worked as an interior photographer and had clients here as well as in London, so the trip seemed like a great idea. I could catch up with my clients and enjoy the Christmas mood in the city.

But now the rabbit had vanished. I read the note ten times, but it didn't give me any more clues. Instead, the words just got blurrier and blurrier in the 3 am silence, disturbed solely by the thoughts in my head. I decided to try to get some sleep and deal with the situation in the morning. I dreamed about rabbits and Athena's owl, chasing them.

The next day, I went to the hotel reception

to see if I could find some answers. The manager said that he hadn't seen anything unusual and promised to check the video footage from the hotel cameras. Noticing my distress, he offered me a complimentary breakfast at the hotel rooftop restaurant.

I sat outside on the roof terrace. Even though it was the nineteenth of December, the weather was still mild. The winter sunrays draped their comforting warmth around me and soothed my mind. I ordered a Freddo Cappuccino with cinnamon and chocolate powder and a salmon and scrambled egg brioche.

The view from the rooftop was mesmerising, certainly one of the best in Piraeus.

On the right, across the marina and the smooth blue sea, sprinkled with the silver glitter of morning light, stretched the Athenian Riviera. On the left, past the Peace and Friendship Stadium and the innumerable white buildings, clustered together, towered the Acropolis and Mount Lycabettus, watching over the great expanse of the city. Low white clouds grazed the edges of the mountains in the distance and an azure blue sky reigned above.

"Kalimera," I heard a voice and looked up, expecting to see the waiter with my order, but to my surprise, I was greeted by the dreamlike face of a man with golden blonde hair, which glowed in the sunlight, and blue eyes that sparkled like sapphires. He wore black jeans, a white t-shirt and a light grey coat that waved in the wind. His whole body radiated a light... a feeling of sunrise and adventure... of life.

"I'm Dionysus. Athena sent me to help you with your task," he said in a voice sweeter than the chocolate powder in my coffee.

"Dionysus," I repeated, suddenly remembering the rabbit and the strange note. It all seemed a bit surreal, but I was beginning to get amused, so I decided to play along. He invited me for lunch at Ilias' Taverna and I accepted. He said he would send a taxi to pick me up at two o'clock. I looked at my watch to check the time, and when I looked back up, he was already gone.

The taxi dropped me off at the taverna and I went inside. The smell of mouth-watering dishes filled the small room and traditional Greek music played in the background. Black and white photographs of boats, fishermen and island scenery decorated the walls. The white-painted wooden chairs and tables, covered with red and white chequered tablecloths, brought freshness to the interior and the sound of animated conversations, clinking of glasses, plates and cutlery created a relaxed atmosphere. I looked at the Christmas tree in the corner by the bar counter. It was an ordinary-looking Christmas tree, covered with multi-coloured baubles of various designs, blue and gold tinsel and lights that flashed in changing patterns. There was no ornament at the top, or maybe I just couldn't see it.

The table closest to the tree was occupied and Dionysus was sitting at the one opposite it. I sat down, and before I even had a chance to look at the menu, he was already ordering—grilled octopus, stuffed calamari, taramosalata, garides saganaki and a carafe of wine. The waiter nodded with approval.

While we were waiting for the food, Dionysus asked me questions about the current work projects I had booked in Athens. He not only spoke to me with the familiarity of a very close friend, but also seemed to know private details about my life. He knew what camera I used for work, which Murakami book was my favourite, and that I usually cooked chicken with green beans on Monday night. Was he a friend of Anastasia? No, he said he hadn't met her.

The food arrived and I realised that I was starving. The calamari were soft and succulent and the plump shrimps juicy with a velvety sauce made from the most flavourful tomatoes, rich with the sweetness of onions and ouzo. The taramosalata was smooth and sharp with the taste of fish roe and lemon. I kept glancing at the tree, in between bites, still unable to locate the ornament at the top.

"If you manage to grab a branch before the tree escapes, you will see the ornament," said Dionysus as if he had read my mind.

Escape? How would the tree possibly escape? And how difficult could it be to grab a branch? I quickly devised a plan. I stood up and walked up to the counter, pretending to need an extra plate. I casually reached towards the tree, but before I could touch it, it turned into a giant snake with scales the colours of the baubles. Red, yellow, blue... they glimmered like stained glass as the creature twirled its body, which glowed as if the snake had swallowed a string of fairy lights. It hissed threateningly, revealing a long gold tinsel tongue, then slid in the direction of the front door, glistening against the surface of the white stone floor as it slithered around the tables and chairs. Skilfully, it threaded around the feet of the man at the door, who was just stepping inside the taverna, and it disappeared outside.

I looked around but no one seemed to have noticed. The waiter greeted the newly arrived customer and handed him the menu, while the laughter and conversations at the other tables continued undisturbed. Dionysus giggled as he looked at me with amusement. The delight on his face was so pure that it made the situation look comic. I sat back at the table and took a big gulp of wine.

"So, what do we do now?" I asked.

"We can enjoy the rest of our lunch and then I will take you somewhere for dessert. The tree will be back by tomorrow evening. It gets homesick quickly," Dionysus responded and took a big bite of the octopus.

The sun was already setting when we

Tigers in Athens

left Ilias' Taverna and headed towards Akti Themistokleous, the road that wove along the sea and contoured the southern coast of Piraeus. When we reached the long row of tavernas, Dionysus stopped and faced the sea. The sun dipped its rays in the water that sparkled like gold coins, while above it, glossy yellow clouds hung from the violet sky. Dionysus raised his arms and started pulling what looked like an invisible string. A small honey-coloured cloud with ruffled grey edges seemed to move closer and closer until it was no further than a foot away from my face.

"It tastes like melomakarona." He took a chunk of the cloud and put it in his mouth.

I gasped. I touched the cloud and tore out a piece. It had the texture of cotton candy and tasted like honey, cinnamon and walnuts—indeed like the Christmas cookies, melomakarona. I was beginning to suspect that Dionysus really was a god. As we walked to my hotel, the stars that decorated the streetlamps broke free and hovered above our heads. Or perhaps it was my imagination. We said goodbye at the hotel reception and arranged to meet the following evening.

The next day passed quickly as I had scheduled a couple of meetings and a photoshoot, so when I got back to the hotel, it was already six in the afternoon. I took a shower and put on a leather skirt and a black top. There was no sign of the rabbit and the empty cage on the floor gave me an eerie feeling. I had to get the Christmas tree ornament.

The taverna was full but Dionysus was already sipping wine at the same table as the day before. The tree was back in its place. We ordered barbounia, the red-coloured fish with sweet flesh, and horta, drizzled with olive oil and lemon juice. Even though the food was delicious, I couldn't stop thinking about the tree. I felt like it was watching us, planning its next move with its pine needles alert.

I decided to order more wine and went up to the counter. Again, the tree was within arm's reach from me, but I didn't look at it. Instead, I looked straight ahead into the small kitchen, where the chef was preparing the food. The bartender came to the counter, and as I ordered, I swiftly tried to grasp the nearest branch. But the tree was no longer there. Instead, a cloud of feathers, green and auburn, golden and dark blue, fluttered in the air. The front door opened, and the cloud moved towards it as if pulled by the wind. Dionysus rushed after it and I followed.

As soon as we stepped outside, the cloud morphed into a giant eagle. With its feet still on the ground, it spread its wings and flapped them as if to check their strength.

"Let's go for a ride." Dionysus pulled me as he jumped onto the eagle's back and clasped its neck. I hopped on and wrapped my hands around Dionysus, just as the eagle lifted us in the air and rose above the five-storey houses. We flew over Piraeus as the ships in the port got smaller and smaller, above the neon blue swimming pool at Pisina, past the yachts at Marina Zeas and the bars opposite them, where the music mixed into a cocktail of unsynchronised noise. We glided above Georgios Karaiskakis Football Stadium and Leoforos Poseidonos, where the cars were just glimmering red and white dots that left traces of light on the road. We flew over the Christmas tree at Syntagma Square until we reached the Acropolis, where the eagle finally descended and disintegrated back into a cloud of feathers that disappeared with the wind. Dionysus laughed and jumped around. Zeibekiko music played from somewhere. He threw himself into a wild dance, swaying and swirling in a trance with his eyes closed, with the light from the Parthenon illuminating his every movement. The next moment, I was dancing beside him, glasses of wine in our hands and snowflakes in the air. Snowing in Athens, dancing with a god on top of the Acropolis... I didn't want this to end. The marble columns were spinning around me, the snowflakes melted in my hands as I spread my fingers to catch them, while Dionysus sang a song about a gipsy. The snow kept falling around us until everything went white.

I woke up in my hotel room with the sunlight caressing my face. The phone was ringing. It was Anastasia, who wanted to check if everything was okay with the rabbit. I told her everything was okay as I didn't want her to worry. I was flying back to London the next day, so I had to retrieve the rabbit fast.

I had a coffee and spent most of the day editing photos on my laptop on the balcony. Occasionally, I took a glimpse at the Acropolis in the distance, still covered in snow, and reminisced about the night before. The phone rang again, but this time, it was Dionysus. He had reserved a table at Ilias' Taverna at eight o'clock. It was my last opportunity to collect the ornament.

I arrived at the taverna ten minutes before eight, but Dionysus was already there, sitting at the table by the Christmas tree. His eyes smiled at the sight of me. We ordered a grilled tsipoura, fried zucchini and a small bottle of ouzo. We savoured the food without hurrying and spoke slowly, taking our time with our words as if we were trying to slow down the limited time we had left together. We drank the ouzo in small sips, hoping to prolong the evening. Our conversation lingered for hours, but as the food on the table diminished, I felt that something was soon going to be irrevocably lost. A voice in my head, perhaps Athena's, reminded me why I was in the taverna and nudged me to act.

I dropped my fork on the floor. The sound of metal falling on the stone floor resonated in the air. I reached down to get it, but instead, I gripped the nearest tree branch. I felt the pine needles lightly prick my fingers. The tree stood immobile as I held the branch in my hand. A gold ornament sparkled at the top. I briskly took it and put it in my handbag. When I turned around, Dionysus was no longer at the table.

I sat down and took a sip of ouzo, my heart still racing with excitement. Fifteen minutes passed, but Dionysus didn't return. I asked the waiter if he had seen my companion, but he said he hadn't, so I asked for the bill. It had already been paid. I waited for another half-hour while I finished my drink, then ordered a taxi back to the hotel.

I sat on the bed and took the ornament out of my pocket. It was a gold statuette of a man holding a glass of wine and seemingly dancing. It was as if time had suddenly stopped and left him frozen in his dance, full of passion. There was something so lifelike in the position of his body that I had the feeling he would move any second. I took a closer look at his face. I recognised the prominent nose, the jawline, the golden hair as if brushed by the wind, and the eyes, full of laughter. It was Dionysus.

I don't know how long I stood motionless with my eyes glued to the statuette. So many

Tigers in Athens

questions ran through my mind, but no answers came. I placed the statuette on the pillow next to mine and turned the light off. A full moon shone outside and bathed the room in silver light. In the monochrome half-light, the statuette still glowed golden.

I woke up to the cry of seagulls. The rosy-cheeked dawn tiptoed quietly in the room. I looked beside me but the statuette wasn't there. I checked under the pillows, in the tangled sheets and under the bed, but I couldn't find it. As I kneeled, I noticed the rabbit, white and fluffy, sitting quietly in its cage, looking at me with curious eyes.

❄ ❄ ❄

I boarded the plane to London and took a seat by the window. A majestic sky, embroidered with fiery orange and vibrant purple clouds, hovered above the runway. The sun melted slowly behind the mountains that shimmered in the distance. Behind my sunglasses, my eyes welled up as I felt this land of gods slowly slip away from me.

"Excuse me, I think you're in my seat," I heard a familiar voice as I took a sip from the water bottle I bought at the airport. But it wasn't water anymore. It was wine, bursting with the luscious aroma of mountain tea, flowers and the sweetness of Greek honey, golden like the smile of Dionysus, whose face glowed in the late afternoon light that streamed from the window.

A strikingly beautiful air hostess with grey eyes walked past and said, "Merry Christmas," as she winked at me. I thought I heard the hoot of an owl.

Printed in Dunstable, United Kingdom